SOCKS
THE BELKNAP MILL CHRISTMAS ELF

Written by
Christopher A. Beyer

Illustrated by
Larry Frates

Socks
The Belknap Mill Christmas Elf
Written by Christopher A. Beyer
Illustrated by Larry Frates

Copyright © 2020 by Christopher A. Beyer. All rights reserved.
Copyright © 2020 illustrations by Larry Frates. All rights reserved.

All rights reserved. This book or any portion thereof may not be reproduced or used in any manner whatsoever without the express written permission of the publisher except for the use of brief quotations in a book review.

Cover art by Larry Frates
Graphic Designer, Pam Marin-Kingsley
Editor, Jane Stucker

Library of Congress Control Number: 2020923947
Paperback ISBN: 978-1-7354250-4-7

Published by:

Contact for More Information:

This book is dedicated to the children of Laconia, New Hampshire.

The Belknap Mill Society thanks Writer, Christopher A. Beyer, Illustrator, Larry Frates, and Publisher, Cathy Waldron. Without their collaboration and talent, this story would not have been possible.

A long time ago, in 1823, when things were much different from the way they are today—when there were no cars being driven, and people had no electricity in their homes—a hosiery mill was built in the City of Laconia, New Hampshire.

What is a hosiery mill you ask? It is a place that makes socks.

This hosiery mill had many workers. They worked hard to make socks for everyone—for those who lived in Laconia, and others near and far. They even made socks for soldiers. These socks were snug, cozy and warm.

One of these hard workers was Mr. J.P. Morin. He made socks for many years, and in 1912, he became the owner of the Belknap Mill. This story is not about him though; it is about his son, Alphonse, and a little elf named…SOCKS!

Alphonse loved Christmas. It was his favorite holiday. Every year he looked forward to hanging up a sock on the mantle so Santa could fill it with gifts and treats.

Then one year as Christmas was approaching, he asked his father, "Can the hard workers at the Mill knit me a special stocking that will make Santa smile with Christmas joy?"

"The Mill workers are already so busy filling orders for socks," his father replied, "and to be honest, I have no idea how to make such a special Christmas stocking. I'm sorry, Alphonse, it can't be done."

It did not seem like he was going to have his wish granted. However, Santa hears every child's wish, and Alphonse would soon find this out.

Socks was a little elf that lived at the North Pole. He was not a toy-making elf like all the others. Oh no—he was a very different kind of elf because he was a tailor. What is a tailor you ask? It is someone who makes, fits, and repairs clothes.

He was very good at what he did. He sewed all the elves' outfits and hats, and made sure Santa's famous red suit was well taken care of. He also made sure Santa, with his big round belly, fit into it every year!

When Santa heard Alphonse's wish, he knew just where to go for help. "Socks, I have something special I would like you to do this year. As you know, children everywhere hang their socks over the fireplace to dry. On Christmas Eve, I fill these socks with wonderful gifts and treats. I would like you to make a special Christmas stocking; one that will bring to me, and to every good little girl and boy, many smiles of Christmas joy."

"And where will I make such a stocking?" Socks asked.

"I have just the place for you. We're going to make a little boy's wish come true," Santa replied.

Santa and Socks went over the details, and the very next evening, on the first of December, Socks paid a visit to the Belknap Mill.

All of the workers had finished their work that day and had gone home, so Socks immediately started to make the special Christmas stocking. He made one, then another, and another.

He worked all through the night. By the time the morning light shone through the Mill's windows, Socks had filled many baskets with red and green stockings.

By now, Socks was very tired, so he found a comfortable place high up in the wooden beams of the Mill and went to sleep.

You can imagine his surprise when Mr. Morin arrived for work that morning and discovered all those stockings. Where had they all come from? He had no idea, but he knew just what he had to do. He gave each of his workers a stocking, and brought one to Alphonse that evening.

When he saw the joy on Alphonse's face, he wanted every child to have one, too.

The very next day, when Mr. Morin arrived at work, there were more baskets of stockings. The days after that, there were more . . . and more . . . and more! For the next three weeks leading up to Christmas, there were baskets of stockings waiting for him every morning. Mr. Morin gave these out to all of his workers' children, and every girl and boy he met.

On December 23rd, Socks had to stop. He needed to return to the North Pole to help Santa prepare for the big Christmas Eve trip.

For over 50 years, Socks returned to the Belknap Mill every December 1st until the Belknap Mill closed down in 1969. It then seemed that there would be no more Christmas stockings made at the Mill ever again, and Socks would remain a Belknap Mill secret.

Recently, children have started to come to the Belknap Mill to learn about its history. With the Mill active again, Socks decided it was time to return—not to make stockings, but to meet the children. Socks now enjoys having fun with all who visit the Belknap Mill every holiday season.

Socks is not a secret anymore. He has become a part of the Belknap Mill's history, a part that all started with a little boy's Christmas wish a long, long time ago.

If you happen to see Socks, be sure to take an "Elfie" with him because he loves photos . . . and he loves seeing children smile.

Also, be sure to thank him for being that special little elf who brought Christmas stocking joy from the Belknap Mill in Laconia, New Hampshire, to children everywhere.

My Elfie Selfie with Socks

ABOUT THE BELKNAP MILL

    The Belknap Mill is the oldest, largely unaltered, brick textile mill in the United States. Built in 1823, it is one of America's oldest surviving textile mills and was a leader in what would become the standard for American manufacturing. The subsequent success of the textile hosiery industry in Laconia and surrounding towns drew inventors and machine manufacturers to Laconia. In 1861, during the Civil War, the Belknap Mill was one of the first mills to convert from weaving to knitting, and through both World Wars the Mill provided socks to our soldiers around the world. Socks continued to be made at the Belknap Mill until 1969. The building was scheduled to be demolished by the City of Laconia as part of a plan to revitalize downtown, when a group of citizens acting under the banner of 'Save the Mill Society,' purchased the building. Because of the national significance of the Mill, the group worked with historic preservationists across the country to save and maintain the building as a cultural community center.

    The Belknap Mill has served as an art and history center and meeting place since being saved in the early 1970's. In a nationally covered scenario, the private nonprofit, cultural organization was the first in the country to be awarded Federal funds as well as recognition from the National Trust for Historic Preservation for preserving an industrial structure.

    Today the Belknap Mill offers a permanent exhibit on industrial history, changing exhibits on art and history, and education programs for adults and children along with workshops, lectures, festivals, and other events, year-round. The Society's programs, preservation projects, community service and management have won national and state awards. The Belknap Mill is known as the Official Meetinghouse of New Hampshire, designated by a former governor for its architectural, geographical, and historical significance.

The Belknap Mill Society operates as a 501(c)(3) nonprofit organization, whose mission is to preserve the Belknap Mill as a unique historic gathering place and to celebrate the Lakes Region's cultural heritage through the arts, education and civic engagement.

About the Author & Illustrator

Christopher A. Beyer was born in Concord, and has lived in NH his entire life. He has been an ESL educator in Laconia, NH, for nineteen years. He currently lives in Penacook, NH, with his two children, a daughter Tristan and a son Trevor. In his free time, he enjoys outdoor activities, writing and coaching track and field.

Larry Frates is the first Artist-in-Residence at the Belknap Mill. His ideas and talents as an artist, educator and magician have made him an important creative catalyst in our community. He very much enjoyed bringing SOCKS to life in this book.

Made in the USA
Monee, IL
24 December 2020